BRIT

DEAD HEAT

ORCHARD BOOKS
338 Euston Road, London NW1 3BH
Orchard Books Australia
Level 17/207 Kent Street, Sydney, NSW 2000

First published in 2015 by Orchard Books
This paperback edition published in 2015
ISBN 978 1 40833 463 8

Text © Shoo Rayner 2015
Illustrations © Shoo Rayner 2015

A CIP catalogue record for this book is available
from the British Library.

1 3 5 7 9 10 8 6 4 2

Printed and bound by CPI Group (UK) Ltd, Croydon, CR0 4YY

Orchard Books is an imprint of Hachette Children's Group
and published by The Watts Publishing Group Limited, an Hachette UK company.

www.hachette.co.uk

Shoo Rayner

ROMAN
BRIT

DEAD HEAT

ORCHARD

FORT FINIS TERRAE
is a sleepy backwater
in the great Roman
Empire. A young
shepherd boy named
Brit lives there with
his sheep and faithful
dog Festus.

INVERNIA

BRITTANICA

FORT FINNIS TERRAE

OCEANUS BRITTANICUS

GALLIA

EURO

NOSTRU MAR

AFRICA

ATLANTICUS
OCEANUS

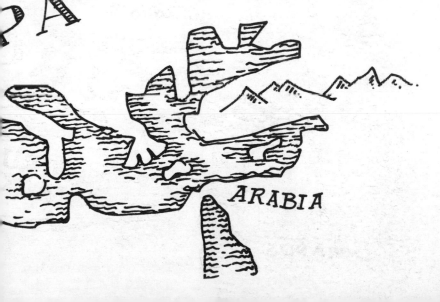

It's a quiet life for Brit and his animals in the fort. But every so often, something happens to make it a day to remember!

GERMANIA

PA

ARABIA

CHAPTER ONE

"I am bored, bored, bored!" sighed
Drusilla. "It's been raining for weeks. I'm
cold, I'm damp and every time I go outside
my hair gets all frizzy!"

"Come and have another game of
knucklebones," said Brit, throwing five
sheep's bones into the air.

He caught them on the back of his hand, lined up in a neat row in the crack between his first and second fingers. "Hey! Peas in a pod!" he cheered. "How good am I?"

"It's so boring playing with you," Drusilla grumbled. "You always win."

While the rain continued to pour outside Brit's barn, there wasn't much else to do. The chickens were roosting in the rafters, quietly clucking to themselves. The sheep were munching their hay, and Brit's dog, Festus, was fast asleep in the corner.

What else could Brit and Drusilla do, but wait for the rain to stop?

"There must be loads of things for you to do at the fort," Brit said hopefully, wondering when Drusilla might think it was time to go home and leave him alone.

Drusilla's father, Gluteus Maximus, was the Commander of Fort Finis Terrae. That meant Drusilla thought she was in charge too.

She had sort of adopted Brit, and thought of him as a bit of a pet.

"Oh, the whole fort is leaking, and Daddy has the soldiers running about with buckets to catch the drips," Drusilla explained. "It's dark, damp and cold. It's much nicer here in your warm, dry barn."

Brit sighed. It looked like Drusilla would be sticking around for a while!

"I wonder if it will EVER stop raining," he said. "The sheep need to get out and eat fresh grass – they'll be having their lambs any day now. Maybe the gods are angry with us. Or maybe they're sad, and can't stop crying, and the rain is their tears."

"Daddy says that Pius Senex, the priest at the temple of Minerva, is waiting for a sign," said Drusilla.

Brit cocked his ear to one side and listened to the rain outside.

"It sounds like it's not coming down quite as hard at the moment," he said. "Why don't we go to the temple and ask the Goddess Minerva to bring some sunshine? We can also ask Pius Senex if he's had his sign yet."

Drusilla nodded and covered her hair with a woollen shawl. "Anything's better than losing another game of knucklebones!"

CHAPTER TWO

The heavy rain had turned into a fine drizzle. There was thick, sticky mud everywhere and the paths were pockmarked with giant puddles. Many of the fields further down the valley were flooded. Ducks and geese swam on ponds and lakes where once there had been green grass.

"Look!" Brit pointed over a hedge. "Can you see them?"

Two hares were standing on their back legs, attacking each other. As they fought, clumps of fur floated through the air.

"What are they doing?" Drusilla whispered.

"They're boxing," said Brit. "That's what they do at this time of year." He rolled his eyes. "They're probably in love. They go a bit crazy – they're mad March hares."

At the sound of the word hare, Festus pricked up his ears. He scrambled through a hole in the hedge and ran towards the startled creatures, barking like a demon.

"You'll never catch them!" Brit laughed.

The two hares split up and ran in opposite directions. Festus chose one of them and chased after it.

"They're much faster than you!" Brit called. The hare was not only fast, it was agile too, twisting and turning with ease.

Eventually, Festus gave up, and limped back to his master, panting.

"You silly thing!" Brit told Festus. The dog's tongue lolled from the side of his mouth as he tried get his breath back.

Suddenly he was off again – yapping and barking at nothing.

Brit chuckled. "Looks like Festus has caught mad March fever too!"

CHAPTER THREE

"Here we are!" said Brit, when they reached the end of the path.

The temple of Minerva stood at the end of the valley. It wasn't very big, for a temple. Pius Senex, the old priest, lived round the back. He said prayers every day, and looked for signs from the gods in the sky and the water. He would warn everyone if there was an omen of bad weather or impending doom.

The face of the
goddess Minerva was
carved into the front
of the temple. Below
the carving there was
a water spout.

Usually, a gentle
stream tinkled and
splashed into the
crystal-clear waters
of Minerva's Pool. Pius would sit and stare
into the water until visions appeared to
him with messages from the gods.

Now, with all the rain, a torrent of water
cascaded from the spout, turning the
surface of the pond into a froth of waves
and bubbles.

"I can't see anything," Pius told them when they asked if he had any news about when the rain might stop. "Maybe you could try making an offering to Minerva?"

When people wanted something badly, they often came and threw coins into Minerva's Pool. The coins would disappear mysteriously overnight. Perhaps Minerva took her gifts…or perhaps that was how Pius paid for things in the market.

"I'm afraid we haven't got any money," said Drusilla.

Pius shrugged. "Never mind," he said. "You can write a message on these pebbles and throw them in the pool for Minerva to read." He gave the children some perfectly round, white pebbles, and darker stones to write on them with.

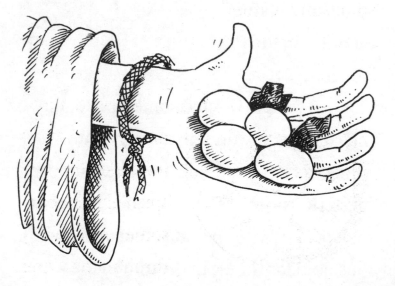

Brit felt his cheeks go hot
with embarrassment.
He couldn't read or
write. "Can I draw a
picture of what I want
instead?" he asked.

"Oh, that's much
better." Pius smiled. "A picture speaks a
thousand words."

Brit scratched an image of a smiling sun

onto his pebble.
He screwed up
his eyes and
imagined the
spirit of Minerva
somehow flowing
through the water.

He concentrated all his thinking to the front of his head, almost sending a beam of thoughts into the pebble.

Dear Minerva, he thought. *Please make it stop raining so my sheep can eat green grass and have lots of lovely new lambs!*

Drusilla did the same, but her wishes were different. *Please, Minerva,* she prayed silently, *can it stop raining so my hair can stop being frizzy?*

Brit pulled back his hand and threw his pebble.

Festus, thinking it was a game, leaped into the air and caught the pebble in his mouth before he crashed into the foaming waters of Minerva's Pool.

"No! Festus! You silly thing! You're not allowed in there! Come back here at once!"

Pius stood with his arms in the air, his mouth making the shape of a perfect O. "Oh! I hope Minerva isn't offended. You never know what she might do. Let's see if she gives us a sign."

Festus paddled to the side of the pool and scrambled out. He dropped the stone at Brit's feet, and looked up at his master with big, brown, faithful, happy eyes.

Then his body began to wriggle and waggle and…a cloud of water sprayed everywhere as Festus shook himself dry.

"No! Festus!" Brit yelled.

"Argh! I'm soaking wet now!" Drusilla cried.

At that exact moment, the clouds parted and a ray of sunlight poured down from the sky. The fine spray of water flew up into the air, creating a beautiful rainbow of brilliant colours all around Festus. He seemed to be surrounded by a halo of multicoloured light.

As soon as Festus stopped shaking, the rainbow disappeared. Brit blinked. Drusilla blinked. Pius blinked.

The clouds seemed to roll away from the sky. Sunshine spread out across the countryside. Birds began singing in the trees. A beautiful, nurturing warmth soaked into their winter-weary bones. It felt like spring had arrived in a mere moment of time.

"Did you just see what I just saw?" Pius
asked in a tone of wonder.

"Y-y-yes!" the children stammered.

"It's a sign!" said Pius, falling to his
knees. "Minerva has sent us a sign. Take
care of your dog, Brit. Minerva has chosen
him as her messenger!"

CHAPTER FOUR

"I don't care if he is Minerva's chosen messenger," Drusilla complained. "I am soaking wet and I smell of dog! I'm going home to get changed."

Brit turned his face to the sun and smiled. Everything was working out just fine after all. "Come on, Festus," he laughed. "There's work to be done."

On the way back to the barn, Festus saw another hare and took off, chasing it around the fields. As ever, the hare was much too fast for him.

As Festus returned to Brit, he suddenly stopped dead in his tracks. He stood motionless, staring at his feet.

"Come on, boy!" Brit called.

But Festus didn't move. The hairs on Brit's arms stood up on end. Festus was standing stock still – had Minerva turned her special messenger to stone?

Brit crept closer. The thing at Festus's feet was almost invisible. Disguised against the brown winter grass, sitting motionless on the ground was a leveret – a baby hare.

Festus gently pawed the tiny creature and whimpered.

Brit turned to go. "Come on, Festus, leave it alone. We've got lots to do. We need to turn the sheep out into the fields."

Festus gently picked up the baby hare in his mouth and followed.

Brit sighed and put his hands on his hips. "Festus, don't be silly! Put it down!"

Brit loved animals, but he had enough to look after already.

Festus looked up at his master. When he looked like that, with his big, brown, pleading eyes, Brit's heart always melted. The baby hare looked at him with big, brown eyes too… double trouble!

"Oh…all right," Brit sighed again. "Bring it along with you if you must, but *you'll* have to look after it!"

Festus, Minerva's messenger, was acting strangely. This was turning out to be a very weird day indeed!

CHAPTER FIVE

By the time Brit and Festus got back to the barn, the mud was already beginning to dry. The chickens were outside, basking in the sunshine, pecking the ground for seeds and juicy worms.

Brit felt he could almost see the new grass growing and the buds on the oak trees exploding into life as bright new leaves clothed their dark frames.

Everywhere birds were singing their hearts out. Flowers, bursting open, called to the bees that hummed lazily over the hedgerows. Spring had finally arrived, chasing away all memories of the long, wet winter.

Festus gently laid his new friend on the fresh green grass and watched, admiringly, as it began to eat.

"He'd better have a name, if he's staying," said Brit. "Let's call him…Lep."

Over the next few weeks, lambs were being born both night and day. Brit watched over his growing flock, making sure that eagles couldn't swoop down from the sky  and carry off a newborn lamb. He kept a fire burning brightly through the night to ward off wolves and foxes that were always on the lookout for fresh, easy meat.

One baby lamb was rejected by his
mother, who already had twins. Brit put it
in a bag across his shoulder and carried it
wherever he went.

*

"Look at you two!" Drusilla laughed.
The spring had turned into summer. It
was hot and Brit's little lamb skipped
behind him and followed him everywhere.

Lep had grown and grown and followed Festus everywhere too.

"I've never seen anything like it," said Drusilla. "Look at them, chasing around the field like that. They're playing together. It's not natural. Festus should have eaten that rabbit a long time ago!"

"It's not a rabbit," Brit said. "It's a hare. But I agree, it is very odd. It's like they're in love with each other! They snuggle up together at night and Lep even helps Festus round up the  sheep. Something very strange happened to Festus the day he jumped into Minerva's Pool!"

And something very strange had happened to the summer. The sun shone on and on and on. No rain had fallen since the day Festus jumped into the pool.

The sun shone brighter and hotter by the day. Soon the fresh green began to turn dry and brown. The muddy paths of spring turned into dusty tracks. The river ran lower and lower.

"Why are those people watching us?" Drusilla asked. It was midsummer's day. Small groups of people huddled together in the shade of the trees near Brit's barn.

"They're waiting for a sign," said Brit, who had noticed the number of people growing day by day. "They want Festus to bring rain. They say that if he stopped it raining in the spring, he can make it start raining again now."

A soldier walked towards them. Bumptius Matius was the chief engineer at Fort Finis Terrae.

"We need rain," he said.

"I know," Brit replied. "There's hardly anything left for my sheep to eat."

Bumptius nodded. "The wells are running dry, and Minerva's spring is reduced to a dribble. If it doesn't rain soon, we will all die of thirst."

"Brit can't make it rain!" Drusilla said crossly.

"No, but his dog can," said Bumptius.  "We've all heard the story. He's Minerva's messenger, and while he spends all his time playing with that rabbit, he's never going to bring us rain. We're all going to die if it doesn't rain soon!"

"Lep's not a rabbit!" Brit said firmly. "He is a hare."

"Rabbit or hare –" Bumptius frowned – "we all think it's time your dog went and asked Minerva for rain."

Brit nodded and thought for a moment. Then he whistled to Festus. "Come on, boy," he called. "Let's go to see Minerva. You'd better bring Lep with you too."

CHAPTER SIX

It was a strange sight. Brit, his lamb,
Drusilla and Bumptius led the way. Festus
and Lep danced around them, chasing
and playing all the way to the Temple of
Minerva. A long line of soldiers and their
families followed in their wake.

A tiny trickle of water dribbled into the pool from the spout beneath Minerva's face. The pool was almost empty. A small fish opened and closed its mouth and slowly slapped the surface of the puddle with its tail.

Pius sat on a stone seat next to the pool. He stared far away into the distance before he noticed the crowd that had assembled.

"Hello! What have we got here, then?" said the priest.

Bumptius hopped uneasily from foot to foot. He wasn't happy being spokesman, but someone had to do something. "We need rain!" he said gruffly. The crowd murmured in agreement.

Pius looked at Festus. "Ah! Here is Minerva's messenger. Maybe he has something to say?"

Festus wondered why everyone was staring at him. He didn't know which way to look. He lay down next to Lep, put his head in his paws and stared up at the sky.

"I don't think he has much to say at all," Brit sighed.

Pius spread his arms towards the pool. "Maybe an offering to Minerva would help?" he said cheerily.

There was more grumbling as people in the crowd pulled out whatever coins they had and tossed them into the pool.

Pius stood
up slowly and
leaned on his
staff. "A sacrifice
must be made."
he announced.
The crowd
murmured in
agreement.

A sacrifice
would be perfect. An animal cooked on
the sacrificial fire would send smoke up
to heaven to tell Minerva how much they
needed it to rain again.

Pius slowly looked around him until
his eyes rested on Festus. Everyone else
followed his gaze.

"Kill the dog!" someone called from the back of the crowd. "He started all this!"

Pius raised his hand. "No! Festus is Minerva's messenger. He should make the sacrifice, not be it. Festus must give us his rabbit, the one thing he truly loves. This will be *his* sacrifice."

Brit gasped! "But, you can't do that!"

"And anyway," said Drusilla, "Lep is a hare, not a rabbit."

Pius walked towards them.

"You can't!" Brit was almost in tears. Festus would be heartbroken if anything happened to Lep. Brit would be heartbroken too. Lep had become part of his life the last few months.

Pius picked up the hare and whispered to Brit. "Come and see me when everyone has gone." He winked and walked  ceremoniously into the temple. No one followed. It was holy in there. Only Pius could go inside.

The crowd held their breath. The silence was only broken by Pius, chanting hymns and prayers as he prepared the sacrifice.

Soon, a thin wisp of smoke appeared from a chimney at the back of the temple and the unmistakeable aroma of roasting meat filled the air.

Festus whined and whimpered. He knew something was terribly wrong.

And then the first wet blob of rain fell right on his nose. Another splashed in the dust and another plopped in the puddle in the pool, making the fish jump.

Seconds later, lightning tore across the darkening sky and a deafening clap of thunder shook the ground.

The crowd cheered and scattered in all directions as huge drops of rain poured

from the sky filling the air with the smell
of hot, wet earth and stone.

"My hair!" screamed Drusilla, running
back towards her home. "It'll go all frizzy!"

*

When the storm was over, Brit and
Festus, followed by Brit's lamb, made
their way back to the temple. Festus was
distraught. He looked for Lep under every
soaking bush.

Already the water was streaming from the spout under Minerva's face and the pool was filled again with crystal-clear water.

Pius was waiting for them. He was stroking something in his arms. Something with long ears. Something that looked a lot like…

"Woof!" As Festus barked, Lep jumped from Pius's arms. Lep and Festus ran to each other, dancing and leaping in the air.

Pius beckoned Brit to sit on the stone seat with him.

"When Festus looked up to the sky, he gave me the sign," Pius explained. "I saw the storm clouds coming behind the  crowd. But I knew they wouldn't be happy without a sacrifice. So Festus and his rabbit helped me out. I wasn't burning a sacrifice, I was just cooking my dinner."

Tears welled up in Brit's eyes. It was so good to see his best friend happy again.

"The crowd will soon forget about Lep," said Pius. "They saw and got what they came for."

"Thank you," said Brit. "And by the way, Lep is a hare, not a rabbit!"

Pius tucked up his tunic, climbed into the pool and began fishing around for the coins the crowd had thrown in.

"Here," said Pius, handing Brit a few of them. "Go and buy Festus a great big bone in the market. I think he's earned it!"

"I will," laughed Brit, hugging his best friend. "Come on, Festus – let's go!"

ROMAN BRIT

COLLECT THEM ALL!

Also available
as an ebook